Disney Junior

Fancy NANCY

What's your Fancy?

Written by
Krista Tucker

Illustrated by
Disney Storybook
Art Team

HARPER
An Imprint of HarperCollinsPublishers

For Addison, who is unquestionably one of a kind!
—Krista

ISBN 978-0-06-284473-6

19 20 21 22 23 SCP 10 9 8 7 6 5 4 3 2 1 ❖ First Edition

Designed by Brenda E. Angelilli and Scott Petrower

Ooh La La!
Mom made butterfly-shaped pancakes!

"Fancy pancakes always taste better," I say.

"I want fancy pancakes too," my little sister, JoJo, says. "I want pirate pancakes!"

"These *are* pirate pancakes," Dad tells her.

"They're shaped like gold coins from a pirate's treasure."

"**Yay!**" says JoJo. "Fancy pirate pancakes!"

"Pirates aren't fancy," I tell my sister.

"They are to JoJo," Dad says.

I like being fancy because it makes me feel unique.
That's fancy for one of a kind.

But I wonder . . . what makes everyone else feel fancy?

"What's your fancy?"

I ask my best friend, Bree.

Bree feels fanciest when she's collecting bugs!

But I think bugs are gross!

"You like bugs too," Bree reminds me.
"A butterfly is a bug!"

Mais oui, of course!

"What's your fancy?"
I ask Mom.

Working in her garden makes Mom feel fancy. She loves planting seeds . . . and watching them grow!

"What's your fancy?"
I ask Dad.

Dad feels fancy when he's fixing antiques.

That's fancy for something old.

Dad makes old things new again. Now we can make new memories with old things.

"What's your fancy?"
I ask my friends Rhonda and Wanda.

"We love soccer!" says Wanda.

"Most of all, we like playing together," says Rhonda.

"What's your fancy?"

I ask my friend Lionel.

Being funny makes him feel fancy.
"Fancy and **egg**cellent!" he jokes.

My neighbor Mrs. Devine is glamorous in a zillion ways!

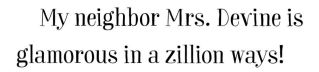

"What's your fancy?"

I ask Mrs. Devine.

She feels fancy when she does the cha-cha! That's a fancy kind of dance.

We both feel fancy anytime we're together.

My dog, Frenchy, adores
when I dress him up. I just add
a few accessories and . . .

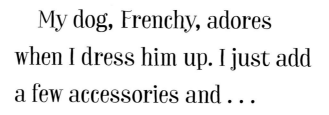

Voilà!

Frenchy feels like the
fanciest dog on the block!

You know, I think nothing feels fancier
than being exactly who you are!